DAVID COPPERFIELD

CHARLES DICKENS

www.realreads.co.uk

Retold by Gill Tavner
Illustrated by Karen Donnelly

Published by Real Reads Ltd
Stroud, Gloucestershire, UK
www.realreads.co.uk

First published in 2007
Reprinted 2010, 2011 (twice), 2012

ISBN 978-1-906230-03-6

Printed in China by Wai Man Book Binding (China) Ltd
Designed by Lucy Guenot
Typeset by Bookcraft Ltd, Stroud, Gloucestershire

CONTENTS

The Characters 4

David Copperfield 7

Taking things further 55

THE CHARACTERS

David Copperfield

David's childhood is shattered
when his mother remarries.
Is he strong enough to find
happiness in spite of the
difficulties he faces?

Peggotty

A loyal servant and friend to
David's mother. For how long will
she be able to help David?

Aunt Betsey Trotwood

David's intimidating aunt.
Will she ever accept him
as her nephew?

Mr Murdstone

David's cruel stepfather. Will he destroy David and his mother?

Steerforth

David's admired schoolfriend. Does he deserve David's trust?

Uriah Heep

Uriah is snake-like in his appearance, but does this mean that David is right to distrust him?

Agnes

Agnes is like a sister to David, who relies upon her support and friendship. Is David being blind?

DAVID COPPERFIELD

That Friday night the storm raged and the wind howled. Rain scratched against the windows, trying desperately to get in. As the clock struck midnight, David's mother cried out with pain. Tiny, pink and naked, David Copperfield was delivered into the world.

As his exhausted mother held him tenderly, he was unaware that the day and time of his birth were bad omens. He was unaware that his father was already dead. He was unaware of the misfortunes and difficulties that lay ahead.

A shrill voice called up the stairs from the parlour, where his Aunt Betsey eagerly awaited the birth of the child, confident that it would be a girl. 'Is she born yet? Come, come, Peggotty, don't dawdle.'

Peggotty, her plump, apple-like cheeks a brighter red than usual, came flustering and

blustering into the parlour from her mistress's room, excited to deliver the news. 'It's a boy!' she gasped. Her bosom swelled with such joy and pride that two buttons popped from her bodice and flew across the room.

Betsey Trotwood silently raised herself from her chair and slowly stooped to pick up her hat. In one fast blast she whacked Peggotty with it. Without a word she marched straight out into the storm, and out of all their lives.

In spite of the ill omens of his birth, the first four years of David's life were happy ones. Loved and guided by his gentle mother and their hard-working servant Peggotty, he grew up honest and trusting, little suspecting how quickly things can change.

Change came one day, in the form of a firm handshake.

'That's the wrong hand, boy.' David looked up. In the face that looked down at him the mouth was smiling, but the cold dark eyes were not. David timidly offered his other hand, and the gentleman grasped it firmly – too firmly for David's comfort.

'Davey, this is Mr Murdstone,' whispered his mother. Jet black hair framed the man's heavy dark face. Standing tall above David, Mr Murdstone blocked out the sun, creating a small patch of shade in which David shivered.

'Pleased to meet you, sir,' he said politely.

'Master Davey,' whispered Peggotty, shaking her head sadly, 'this is your new pa.'

That one simple sentence heralded the end of David's life as he had known it.

Murdstone was a firm believer that children had to be handled with firmness, and kept a safe distance from their parents.

'Be firm, Clara,' he told David's mother whenever she showed any desire to embrace, kiss or laugh with her son. 'Be firm, my dear,' he said when she tried to comfort David in his new loneliness.

David's mother begged Murdstone not to beat her son, and cried when David was dragged, terrified, from the room. Peggotty followed, trying in vain to pull Murdstone back.

'Oh, pray don't beat me, sir!' cried David. 'I do try to be good! I only wanted to talk to my mother. Oh please!'

David felt that the beating would never end. He was torn and bleeding, his face red with fury and fear. Whack! The pain was unbearable. Whack! He had to act quickly. Whack! Turning his head, he desperately sank his teeth deep into Murdstone's arm.

The inevitable punishment followed. The room in which Murdstone locked David was

dark and dusty. For five days David sat alone,
longing to weep in his mother's arms. His only
visitor was Peggotty, who delivered his daily
rations of bread and water.

On the fifth evening, a gentle tapping at his
door woke David from dreams of his mother's
smile. He crept across the room. Surely, at last,
his mother had come to forgive him, to tell
him she still loved him. He could hear sobbing
outside the door. Peeping through the keyhole,
David saw only the tearful face
of Peggotty.

'Oh Master Davey,' she
sobbed. 'They are sending
you away to school.'

The following
morning, manhandled
by Murdstone into the
awaiting coach, David
had no time to bid his
mother farewell.

She was crying as Murdstone held her firmly in his arms, his eyes shining with malice. 'Be firm, Clara, be firm,' he reminded her.

As the coach pulled away, Peggotty burst from the garden and handed David a bag of

warm scones. 'You must never forget me as I'll never forget you, Master Davey. I'll take great care of your mother.'

David felt his breast swell with love for Peggotty. As his beloved home and his childhood happiness disappeared over the horizon, he opened the paper bag. With the scones was a note: 'For Davey, with my love. Mama.'

The high brick walls of Salem School gave it a prison-like appearance. Inside, boys' energetic voices faded to forlorn echoes in the dreary classrooms. Young faces that should have been glowing were as white as ashes, and young hearts that should have been flying amongst birds had sunk to the bottoms of boys' boots.

Since his arrival two days ago, David had been forced to wear a sign around his neck saying, 'Beware: it bites'.

'Does it really bite?' laughed one boy, poking David with a cruel finger. 'Here Fang!' laughed another, 'Here, you ferocious dog!'

'Stop this!' commanded a confident voice. Looking up through his tears, David saw the handsome face and curling hair of a boy about six years his senior. David thought that this must be his guardian angel.

The boy removed David's sign. 'James Steerforth,' smiled the boy, holding out his hand like an adult. 'I'll take care of you.'

Steerforth's next act of friendship was to use the money from David's pocket to buy all the boys some sweets. The boys and David loved him for this. David looked up to Steerforth with gratitude and admiration.

Life in Salem School was cruel. The boys were far too troubled and knocked about by the

teachers to learn anything. David found comfort
in the occasions when Steerforth did him the
honour of talking to him in the playground, or
of asking him to read stories at night.

Whenever gifts arrived from Peggotty –
cakes, sweets, books or money – David handed
them willingly to Steerforth. Once, when
Steerforth allowed him to keep Peggotty's
cordial to moisten his mouth whilst he read to
him, David almost wept with gratitude.

The weeks and months passed as weeks and months always do. The school holidays crept ever closer, until the joyful day arrived. David's smile was fresher and his step lighter than anyone's as he climbed into the coach to sit next to Peggotty. They set off for her brother's home at the seaside.

'Tell me about your school, Master Davey.'

'No, Peggotty. Please tell me about Mr Peggotty, Ham and Little Em'ly.'

Peggotty described her family with such love and pride that, when they finally arrived in Yarmouth, David felt that he had known them all his life. The boat on which Mr Peggotty lived with his two adopted children was just as interesting, homely and comfortable as Peggotty had described. Ham, a boy of about David's age, was just as handsome, strong and friendly, and Little Em'ly just as pretty, as the pictures painted in David's mind.

'So, you be Mas'r Davey,' smiled the
bearded, weather-beaten Mr Peggotty. 'Welcome
to our home. Little Em'ly, take Mas'r Davey to
see the sea out yonder. I want to talk to my
dear sister.'

Each day, David and Emily walked hand-in-
hand along the beach, throwing stones into the
breaking waves.

'I'm afraid of the sea,' confided Emily. 'It can be very cruel. I have seen it tear big boats apart, and it killed my father.'

'But it seems so beautiful,' said David. 'I should like to stay by the sea all my life.'

'And I should like to move away,' answered Emily. 'I want to be a fine lady.'

In the warmth of this little family, whose hearts were as good as gold and as true as steel, the week passed all too quickly.

'Visit again soon!' called Emily as the coach carrying David and Peggotty turned away from the sea and headed back to the place of David's lost childhood.

David was shocked to see his mother looking frail and ill, but the small baby she held in her arms, his own new brother, filled him with delight. The delight was multiplied a hundred

times when he learned that Mr Murdstone was away on business.

David could not know that his memories of this week with his mother, brother and Peggotty would be the most bittersweet he would ever possess. They walked together, sang songs, and wept with joy and with sorrow. His mother's trembling hand stroked David's hair whilst he held his precious baby brother tenderly, and Peggotty looked after them all. Without Mr Murdstone's brooding presence they all blossomed in the spring light. The only cloud in the April sky was David's realisation that his mother's fear of Murdstone was even greater than his own.

That heavenly week came to an end all too soon. His vision blurred by tears, the last thing David saw was his mother, pale-faced and weeping, holding her baby high in the air so that David might wave him farewell. As the coach disappeared she collapsed into Peggotty's arms. 'Something tells me I shall never see my darling boy again. God bless my fatherless Davey.'

Back in school, just three weeks later, the news was delivered to David as abruptly as I shall deliver it here. 'Your mother is dangerously ill,' said the headmaster. 'In fact, she is dead. So is her baby. You must go home.'

Bidding farewell to Steerforth and the other
boys, David left Salem's grey walls for ever.
With deep grief and dread he walked into his
old home, now turned cold and loveless by
Murdstone. Peggotty's warm, loving arms were
waiting for him.

'They faded slowly away,' Peggotty told him gently when they had no more tears to shed. 'Murdstone wore her down until there was nothing left. She died in my arms. Your poor little brother followed the next day. I promised I would take care of you, but Murdstone has discharged me. Tomorrow, straight after the funeral, I must leave for Yarmouth. You are to stay here with Murdstone. Be strong, Master Davey, be constant, be good.'

Peggotty thought for a while, then said, 'Your only living relative is your father's sister, your Aunt Betsey Trotwood, who lives in Dover. I sometimes wonder— ' She did not finish this thought. Instead she said, 'Remember though, Master Davey, I will always keep a room for you in Yarmouth.'

With his mother, brother and father deep in the ground, and Peggotty far away, there was nobody left to bring light into David's dark world. Murdstone detested his presence and David was miserable in his old home. The usual joys of a boy's childhood were unknown to David. He grieved for all the people who had passed from his life and he sometimes wondered what Peggotty had wanted to say about the mysterious Aunt Betsey.

It was only a matter of time before
Murdstone found a way to get rid of David
– he sent him to London to work in one of the
factories from which he had made all his money.
Poorly paid and cruelly treated, David lodged
with a warm-hearted but desperately poor family,
and learned the hard way all about debt, poverty,
hunger, sorrow and hopelessness.

As the seasons passed and life grew ever
harder, the seed planted by Peggotty began to
grow a shoot. David began to wonder about
Aunt Betsey Trotwood who, so the story went,
had so wanted him to be a girl that she had hit
Peggotty with her hat on the day of his birth. A
resolve gradually formed in David's mind. He
would go to Dover to find Aunt Betsey. She was
his only hope.

For six desperate days David bravely tramped alone along the long, long road. He was robbed, beaten and deceived, drenched by downpours and blasted by the wind. Finally, hungry, ragged and exhausted, he reached Dover's white cliffs.

'I'll show you where she lives,' offered a coachman, 'but she's a fearsome woman.'

Fear had become David's familiar companion, and he felt it again when Aunt Betsey opened her front door, looked down at him, and snapped, 'Go away! No boys here!'

David blinked up at her hostile face. His clothes were torn, his skin, of which plenty was now revealed, was sunburnt and dirty, his bare feet were blistered.

'If you please Aunt – I am your nephew.'

'My what? Oh Lord!'

Aunt Betsey turned a shade of grey to match her neatly-combed hair and immediately sat down on the floor, where she remained at David's feet for several minutes. Recovering herself, she dashed indoors. First covering her sofa to protect it from his dirt, she told David to lie down. 'I should feed it,' she told herself, 'even though it is a boy.'

She flustered back from the kitchen with a selection of liquids for David: aniseed water, salad dressing, brandy and fish sauce. Pouring them down his confused throat, she told herself, 'I should wash it, even though it's a boy.'

So David was scrubbed, rubbed and powdered until he shone and smelt of flowers. Having only her own clothes in the house, Aunt Betsey wrapped her nephew in a long lavender dress and purple shawl. 'I should let the poor boy sleep now.'

As David slept his first real sleep for a week, he thought he felt a gentle hand stroking his hair, and he thought he heard his aunt's voice whispering, 'Poor fellow. He looks just like his father.'

David was woken by an unusual alarm call. 'Mercy on us! Donkeys! Donkeys!' cried Aunt Betsey, darting from her house to chase some stray donkeys from her tidy lawn. The same thing happened every morning. Armed with a long stick, Aunt Betsey was ferocious in defence of her precious grass.

On the fourth day, Mr Murdstone arrived to take David back home. Unaware of the danger he faced, he rode his jet black horse

onto the sacred patch of lawn. He thus
confirmed himself in Aunt Betsey's mind as a
man capable of any evil. Terrified by the sight
of a snarling lady waving a stick, followed by
a boy in a flowery lavender dress, he turned
his horse and fled. 'Murderer!' shrieked Aunt
Betsey after him. 'Go away, or I'll knock your
hat off. The boy is staying with me.'

'Well, David dear,' smiled Aunt Betsey a few weeks later. 'I think we have both recovered from the shock of meeting each other. You need to continue your education. We must find you the best school in town.' Three weeks later, his lavender dress exchanged for a smart suit, David embarked upon his second school career. 'Be a fine, firm fellow with a will of your own,' Aunt Betsey told him.

Dr Strong's school was everything a school should be. The kindest of men, Dr Strong treated his students with respect and trust. In response, they studied hard and behaved like gentlemen.

In order to be nearer the school, David moved to live with Aunt Betsey's accountant, Mr Wickfield, and his lovely daughter Agnes. Having learned very little at Salem School, David discovered that he was behind the other boys in his learning, even though he had experienced so much more of life. Through determined study,

and with the patient, gentle help of Agnes and
her father, he made rapid progress.

'Are you happy, dear David?' asked Aunt
Betsey on one of her visits. 'I am very happy
indeed,' replied David.

A fourth person lived in Mr Wickfield's
house: his clerk, Uriah Heep. The first time
David shook Uriah's hand, it felt as though
he was holding a slithering snake. Piercing
green eyes peered through pale eyelashes.

David's eyes were drawn to his short-cropped hair and his smirking mouth. Uriah's whole body seemed to writhe like a snake. He even hissed a little when he spoke. 'I am so pleased to meet you,' he squirmed. 'For a very 'umble person like me this is a great honour. I am the 'umblest person going. 'Umble I am, 'umble I 'ave ever been, 'umble I shall stay.'

David walked away, trying to rub the uncomfortable memory of Uriah's handshake from his hand. It was like trying to wipe off slug-slime.

The years passed happily, and David grew into a young man. Wickfield and Agnes kept a calm home in which David flourished. Agnes became like a sister to him, in whose presence he felt very comfortable.

'You are so good, so calming and sweet-tempered,' he told her on his final day of school. You have helped me like no one else. Can I help you? I fear that something is troubling you and your father, and I think that it involves Uriah Heep.'

Agnes put her hands over her eyes. It was the first time David had ever seen her cry, and it grieved him terribly. 'Oh David,' she whispered, 'Uriah is going to enter into partnership with Papa.'

'That snake! You must not allow it! You cannot trust him!'

'But Papa is afraid of him. He has a powerful hold over Papa.'

David held Agnes more tightly. Looking up into his eyes, she pleaded with him, 'If you want to help me, please be friendly to Uriah.'

As the weeks passed, Uriah's influence coiled ever tighter around Mr Wickfield. Respecting Agnes' request, David overcame his disgust to remain on friendly terms with Uriah. One evening Uriah followed him to his room.

''Umble as I am, I should be proud of a chance to talk with you,' he writhed at David's door. David let him slither in, sat him down, and asked him straight out: 'Uriah, is it your intention to take over Mr Wickfield's business?'

'Oh no. An 'umble person like me had better not aspire. I must stay 'umble if I am to get on in life. I am here to talk to you of other things.' Looking piercingly into David's face, Uriah hissed, 'Don't you find my Agnes beautiful? I worship the ground my sweet Agnes walks on.'

David swallowed hard. 'What makes you think you can call her "my Agnes"?'

'Because when I am ready, Master David, she shall be mine.'

David felt sick, so sick that he had to ask his squirming guest to leave.

The time came for David, now aged seventeen,
to look for work, and he moved to London.
One evening, sitting alone in a tavern, he felt a
warm hand on his shoulder. Turning swiftly, he
saw a familiar, smiling face, framed by curls.
'My God! It is you! It's little Copperfield!'

    'Steerforth!' gasped David, joyfully
surprised by this chance reunion with his old
school friend.

They chatted about old times, and about the paths their lives had taken since they last met. David's story was of poverty and hard work, Steerforth's of wealth and idleness.

'Steerforth, next month I will visit Peggotty and her family in Yarmouth. Do you remember that I once told you about them? Would you like to come with me?'

'Ah, the sailor family. I suppose a visit could be amusing.'

David wasn't paying attention. He had had another idea. 'First, though, you must meet my dear friend Agnes; I will arrange it.'

When he met Agnes, Steerforth was handsomely charming and polite. David marvelled at his natural gift of adapting himself to whomsoever he pleased, and seeming interested in all that concerned them. Glowing with pride, David seized his first opportunity to hear Agnes's praise of his friend. 'Agnes, my angel. Don't you find Steerforth a fine fellow?'

Slowly she replied, 'As I am your good angel, I must warn you about your bad angel. David, I am afraid you have made a dangerous friend.'

'What can you possibly mean?' gasped David, horrified.

'Don't trust him, David.'

David was shocked. Their opinions had never differed before. He felt irritated. 'Who are you to judge a man's character? You, who are letting the snake Heep slither all over your home; you who will one day marry him!'

Pale and trembling, Agnes whispered, 'I shall never marry Uriah. I shall never marry anybody unless I love them more than anybody else in the world.' She looked up at David. 'Do not be blind about Steerforth.'

The following months passed swiftly. David and Steerforth spent a happy time with Peggotty and her family in Yarmouth. Back in London, David found a job with a legal firm. His employer's sweet daughter, Dora, with her childlike manners and long dark hair, captured David's heart so that he thought of little else. This exciting whirlwind of activity blew Agnes and her warning almost completely from David's mind.

One bright morning there was a knock on the door of David's lodging. He was surprised to see Mr Peggotty, agitated and deathly pale. 'Oh Mas'r Davey,' sighed the stricken man, 'Little Em'ly's run away. She has brought ruin and disgrace upon herself. She has run away with a man. She hopes he will marry her and make her a lady. He will not. I know he will not. She is ruined.'

Fingers of fear began to wrap around David's heart. 'Mr Peggotty, who is this man?'

Mr Peggotty paused, looking carefully at David's worried face. 'The damned villain is your friend, Steerforth.'

In the back of his mind David heard Agnes' warning words. He had ignored them, and had introduced heartbreak into the happy Yarmouth home. He knew that Mr Peggotty was right: Steerforth would never make Emily a lady.

'Ham and I will search for her until the day we die,' said Mr Peggotty with determination. 'We will recover Little Em'ly.'

David and Mr Peggotty rushed back to
Yarmouth that same day. When they reached
the beach, doom-laden clouds were advancing
across the darkening sky, and the wind had
launched its assault.

They found Ham amongst a crowd of

people staring out to sea. A boat, smashed on the rocks, was rapidly being swallowed by the hungry sea. One man clung desperately to its sinking mast.

David suddenly realised that Ham was striding into the sea, his determined eyes fixed upon the desperate sailor.

The crowd watched in awed silence as a wave, big enough to engulf the whole town, crashed high above Ham's head. When the wave roared triumphantly to the shore, it carried Ham's body with it. His generous heart was stilled forever.

David later heard that Steerforth had grown tired of Emily and abandoned her. Mr Peggotty and his adopted daughter were unable to resume their idyllic seaside existence. They decided to start a new life in far away Australia.

More bad news followed. A week after his sorrowful return to London, David opened his door to a pale and anxious Aunt Betsey.

'I'm afraid I'm ruined, my dear. Our money has gone.'

'Gone?' asked David, 'Gone where?'

'I invested unwisely. Mr Wickfield was looking after my investments and I'm afraid I made some unlucky decisions. We must meet our ill fortune boldly. I shall have to learn to live more frugally, and can no longer afford to give you an allowance.'

David accepted that without his aunt's support he could no longer afford to live in London. He explained his new poverty to Dora's family. Shunned by her father, he returned to Dover to live with Aunt Betsey and mend his broken heart.

'Dora is a lovely girl, David, but were you not blind?' asked Aunt Betsey, attempting to comfort her forlorn nephew.

'Blind, Aunt Betsey? Dora is beautiful. She is so childlike, so lighthearted and so lovely.'

'She is silly and light-headed,' said Aunt Betsey gently. 'Your young love would soon have burnt itself out. Find somebody who will stand alongside you in both joys and troubles, a true friend and equal.'

'I know no such person.'

'Ah David. Blind, blind, blind.'

Eager to see old friends, David made frequent visits to Mr Wickfield and Agnes. Agnes' serenity was like medicine to David's aching heart and mind. He began to look forward to seeing her with excitement, but also with fear. Could this be what his aunt had been suggesting? Agnes was so true, so beautiful, so dear to him, but had she not told him that she would never marry? He – poor, foolish and blind – was surely not worthy of her love.

Gentle Agnes rarely mentioned the decline of her father's health and business, rarely referred to Uriah Heep's control over their lives.

Meanwhile, Aunt Betsey was busy. Whilst David and Agnes talked, Aunt Betsey spent hours with Mr Wickfield, checking his accounts, his receipts and all the details of his work. Scared of Aunt Betsey, Uriah Heep stayed in the shadows, watching with his sharp little eyes.

Finally, armed with evidence a-plenty,
Aunt Betsey was ready to confront Uriah.
'Heep,' she told him, 'you have deceived your
employer. You have been his torturer. You have
stolen his reputation and his peace of mind.
You have taken his money, my money, and that
of many others too.'

Uriah squirmed uncomfortably, but
remained silent.

'Good Lord, man!' exclaimed Aunt Betsey
impatiently. 'Are you a man or a snake? If
you're a man, control your limbs! I am not
going to be serpentined out of my senses.'

Once Uriah had been unmasked and his thieving exposed, he was a ruined man. While he languished in prison, Mr Wickfield's fortunes steadily improved. Aunt Betsey recovered a small portion of her lost investments; just enough, combined with an income from David's work, to allow them both to live comfortably. David was relieved that Agnes and her father were free from Uriah's venomous influence, but still felt unworthy of her affection.

David now had regular work as a writer and journalist; though he had fewer excuses to visit Agnes, David wrote to her regularly. She always replied in a brief but friendly way, and though he tried to be satisfied with her sisterly love he searched for signs of any greater affection in her letters.

One day he received a long letter in which Agnes expressed particular pride and joy in his achievements. She said that she would always love and support him wherever he went and whatever he did. This gave David the courage he needed to visit her.

Carrying the letter in a pocket close to his rapidly-beating heart, David knocked nervously on the familiar front door. Agnes' beautiful face

lit up when she saw David, but there was sadness in her smile as she led him inside.

David was so nervous he could barely talk. 'Tell me of yourself, Agnes,' he began awkwardly. 'You have hardly ever told me of your own life in all this space of time.'

'What should I tell?' she replied, 'You know all.'

'All, Agnes?'

She looked at him, then turned to leave the room, close to tears. David stopped her.

'Dearest Agnes, whom I so respect and honour, whom I so devotedly love. Please tell me, will I ever be able to call you something infinitely more precious than sister?'

Agnes's tears began to fall. David held her close and told her, 'You were always so much wiser than me, and I was always so in need of your guidance and support. I took for granted that I could rely on and confide in you. I failed to notice how much I loved you.'

Agnes laid a gentle hand on David's shoulder. 'David, there is one thing I must say.'

'Dearest, what is it?'

'Do you not know?'

'I am afraid to guess.'

'I have loved you ever since we first met.'

They were married within a fortnight. Peggotty, Aunt Betsey and Mr Wickfield were full of joy as Mr and Mrs Copperfield's carriage pulled away from the church.

Sitting with his good angel clasped in his arms, David looked back on his life. He remembered boyhood happiness curtailed; a short, precious time with his mother and brother; friends both dear and false. He saw an image of a boy, penniless, battered and bruised, finally arriving in Dover, carrying in his breast a heart that would one day belong entirely to Agnes.

TAKING THINGS FURTHER

The real read

This *Real Reads* version of *David Copperfield* is a retelling of Charles Dickens' magnificent work. If you would like to read the full novel in all its original splendour, many complete editions are available, from bargain paperbacks to beautifully-bound hardbacks. You may well find a copy in your local charity shop.

Filling in the spaces

The loss of so many of Charles Dickens' original words is a sad but necessary part of the shortening process. We have had to make some difficult decisions, omitting subplots and details, some important, some less so, but all interesting. We have also, at times, taken the liberty of combining two events into one, or of giving a character words or actions that originally belong to another. The points below will fill in some of the gaps, but nothing can beat the original.

- Mr Murdstone has a sister, Miss Murdstone, who helps him to make David's life unbearable. His easily-influenced mother follows their heartless guidance in her treatment of David.

- Peggotty marries a colourful character called Barkis, who dies towards the end of the novel.

- At Salem House, David makes another friend called Tommy Traddles. Good-natured Traddles is the victim of bullying by both the boys and the teachers. He returns later in the novel and plays an important role in the plot. He is always admirable and honest.

- Dickens introduces readers to the mothers of both Uriah Heep and Steerforth. Neither is a good example of parenting.

- Little Em'ly and Ham are engaged to be married when Emily elopes with Steerforth.

- When Ham drowns trying to save the man from a sinking ship, nobody knows that the man is Steerforth, whose body is eventually washed up on the shore. David doesn't tell Mr Peggotty and Emily about Ham's death.

● Aunt Betsey's constant companion is Mr Dick. Most people consider him mad, but she relies upon his judgement and he is a good friend to David.

● Dr Strong and his wife, Annie, are also victims of Uriah's scheming, but their happiness is eventually restored by Mr Dick.

● The family David lives with in London is called Micawber. Mr and Mrs Micawber are wonderful characters, always struggling with debt but always optimistic and loyal.

● Dora is a delightful girl, and everybody is fond of her. While David is still with Dora, Agnes and Dora become friends. Aunt Betsey calls her 'Little Blossom'.

● Dora marries David in spite of his poverty. She asks him to call her his 'child-wife'. Their love is real, but David becomes aware of limitations to their relationship. Dora dies an early death, telling Agnes that she wants her to be David's next wife.

Back in time

David Copperfield is Dickens' most autobiographical novel. When Dickens was twelve years old, his father was sent to a debtor's prison. The young Charles had to work in a warehouse to earn money for the family. David's career follows the same pattern as Dickens' – law clerk, journalist, novelist.

Victorian England was in a period of great transition. Having been an agricultural, rural economy, it was moving swiftly towards industrial nationhood. A 'middle class' was emerging, with considerable economic and political influence. However, the divide between the rich and the poor was quickly widening. Dickens shows the weak position of poor people. David Copperfield is only saved and allowed an education because Aunt Betsey is wealthy.

The majority of Victorian children did not receive a formal education. It was not until 1891 that they were entitled to free state education. Through the difference between Salem School and Mr Strong's school, Dickens shows that cruelty and parrot-fashion learning are ineffective compared with education that enables students to develop their imaginations and morals in a caring environment.

Finding out more

We recommend the following books and websites to gain a greater understanding of Charles Dickens' and David Copperfield's England:

Books

- Terry Deary, *Loathsome London* (Horrible Histories), Scholastic, 2005.

- Terry Deary, *Vile Victorians* (Horrible Histories), Scholastic, 1994.

- *Victorian London,* Watling Street Publishing, 2005.

- Ann Kramer, *Victorians* (Eyewitness Guides), Dorling Kindersley, 1998.

- John Malam and David Antram, *You Wouldn't Want To Be a Victorian Schoolchild: Lessons You'd Rather Not Learn,* Hodder, 2002.

- Mandy Ross, *Victorian Schools* (Life in the Past), Heinemann, 2005.

- Peter Ackroyd, *Dickens*, BBC, 2003.

Websites

- www.victorianweb.org
Scholarly information on all aspects of Victorian life, including literature, history and culture.

- www.bbc.co.uk/history/british/victorians
The BBC's interactive site about Victorian Britain, with a wide range of information and activities for all ages.

- www.dickensmuseum.com
Home of the Dickens Museum in London, with details about exhibits and events.

- www.dickensworld.co.uk

Dickens World, based in Chatham in Kent, is a themed visitor complex featuring the life, books and times of Charles Dickens.

- www.charlesdickenspage.com

A labour of love dedicated to Dickens, with information about his life and his novels. Many useful links.

- www.bbc.co.uk/history/trail/victorian_britain

A site offering source materials and guidance in how to use them, as well as a wealth of information.

Food for thought

Here are some things to think about if you are reading *David Copperfield* alone, or ideas for discussion if you are reading it with friends.

In retelling *David Copperfield* we have tried to recreate, as accurately as possible, Dickens' original plot and characters. We have also tried to imitate aspects of his style. Remember, however, that this is not the original work; thinking about the points below, therefore, can help you begin to understand Charles Dickens' craft. To move forward from here, turn to the full-length version of *David Copperfield* and lose yourself in his wonderful storytelling.

Starting points

- Which character interests you the most? Why?

- How surprised were you when Steerforth betrayed David's trust?

- How does the reader know that David should not trust Uriah Heep?

- What qualities can you find in the characters of David and Aunt Betsey?

- Compare David's attraction towards Dora with his love for Agnes.

Themes

What do you think Charles Dickens is saying about the following themes in *David Copperfield*?

- families
- education
- poverty and wealth
- trust and betrayal
- love

Style

Can you find paragraphs containing examples of the following?

- descriptions of setting and atmosphere
- repetition of sounds (assonance and alliteration) to create rhythm and enhance description
- the use of imagery to enhance description
- the use of humour

Look closely at how these paragraphs are written. What do you notice? Can you write a paragraph in the same style?

Symbols

Writers frequently use symbols in their work to deepen the reader's emotions and understanding. Charles Dickens is no exception. Think about how the symbols in this list match the action in *David Copperfield*.

- the sea
- angels
- light and shadow